First U.S. Edition

Library of Congress Cataloging-in-Publication Data

Butterworth, Nick.
  Nice or nasty.

  Summary: Animal and human characters introduce
opposite concepts such as fast and slow, wet and dry,
weak and strong.
  1. English language – Synonyms and antonyms – Juvenile
literature. [1. English language – Synonyms and
antonyms] I. Inkpen, Mick. II. Title. III. Title:
Book of opposites.
PE1591.B8 1987 428.1 86-27455
ISBN 0-316-11915-6

Printed in Italy

NICE OR NASTY

A BOOK OF OPPOSITES

NICK BUTTERWORTH AND MICK INKPEN

Little, Brown and Company
Boston   Toronto

Black and white

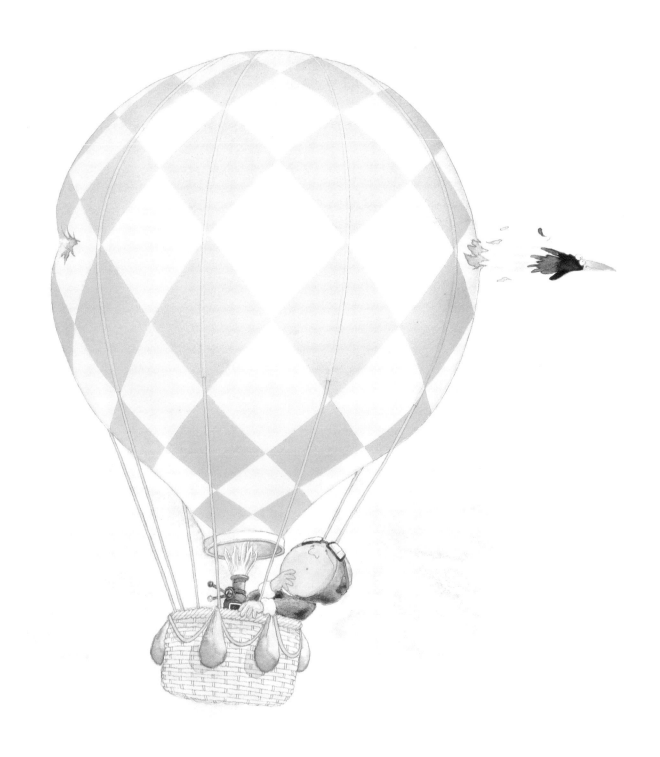

Fast and slow

Up...

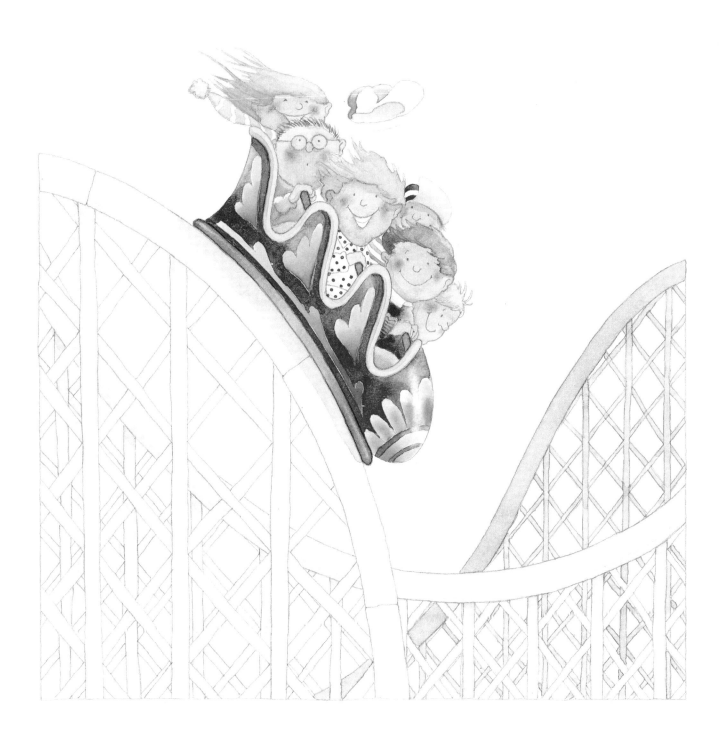

and down

Big and little

Quiet and loud

First…

and last

Nice and nasty

Fat and thin

Hot...

and cold

Hard and soft

Long and short

On...

and off

Rough and smooth

Weak and strong

Day...

and night

Wet and dry

Old and new

Shut and open